For my Mom who filled my childhood with love and happy memories.
And
For Sadie the Bear: dog of my life, kindred spirit, my magical best friend.
~K.P.

For my Mom for her unconditional love and support.
~K.S.

First Edition 2005

Library of Congress Card Number 2005904173

ISBN 0-9769750-0-9

Published in the United States

Printed in China

Graphic Design by indigraphics, Northampton, MA

The illustrations in this book were done in colored pencil, pen and watercolor.

Yaboo Books
PO Box 113929
North Providence, RI 02911
Visit us at: ***www.SadieTheBear.com***

Sadie the Bear

by Kathryn Priestley

illustrated by Karen A. Schroeder

narrated by Maureen Moran

On a warm summers night,
With a harvest moon,
Four weeks after
the month of June,

Come what may,
come what might,
A shooting star
streaks across the sky

And in her hands,
from an angel's lair,
Lay a small black pup,
named Sadie the Bear.

A pup named “Bear”,
Now how could that be?

A bear is a cub
not a small puppy.

But Sadie was born
in the northern sky,

JOY
LOVE
Peace
RUN
JUMP
PLAY

She dropped from the stars
as the night slid by.

From the western side of Ursa Major,
The sign of the Bear,
Where the angels laid her.

Sprinkled in moon dust
and magical fare,
Down from the heavens came
Sadie the Bear.

Kindness and goodness
were hers from the start.
Courage and laughter
filled up her heart.
N
W
E
S
SADIE

Happiness followed
wherever she roamed,
My house was the place
that Sadie called home.

She came into my life
when she was a pup.

In the course of a year
my Sadie grew up.

During that time
I came to believe,
Sadie could do
incredible things!

She'd jump
and she'd run,
JOY
LOVE
Peace
RUN
JUMP
PLAY

And growl like a bear,

N
W
E
S
And wagging her tail
she'd fly through the air!

Over the trees and into the clouds,
Adventures aplenty awaiting her now.

At night she comes home
to sleep on my bed.

With a scratch of her ears
and a kiss on her head,

I whisper, “Sweet Dreams,
sleep warm and take care.
I love you the most,
my Sadie the Bear.”

Sadie the Bear

2000 miles down the road
Just to find myself fighting off the cold
13 months come and gone
Lost in the woods without a map
Nothing looks familiar looking back
I button up my coat and move along

Chorus: And I find myself on the outside looking in, grinnin'
Thoughts become steam in the air
Now I'm shaking off the cold, growin' just a little older
And right beside me - Sadie the Bear

Side by side on the trail
Body achin', winds begin to wail
We huddle close and push against the storm
Peerin' through the darkness for a light
Frozen fear accompanies the night
But Sadie's always there to keep me warm

Chorus:

Back on the road once again
Never sure what waits around the bend
Shinin' sun or fallin' snow
Smilin' faces few and far between
Miles behind us doesn't change a thing
With Sadie here I always have a home

Chorus:

Sweet Dreams

Close your eyes, go to sleep
All warm & safe
Tomorrow brings special things
A happy new day
Close you eyes, go to sleep
Dear little one
Sleepytime's beckoning
Gone is the sun
I will stay close to you
Holding you tight
Whisper "Sweet dreams Love"
And kiss you good night

Bridge:
Oh the moon and the stars above
Will sing you their lullaby
Filled with the warmth of love
Your heart and my heart will shine

Close your eyes, go to sleep
All warm & safe
Tomorrow brings special things
A happy new day
I will stay close to you
Holding you tight
Whisper "Sweet dreams Love"
And kiss you good night

Author **Kathryn Priestley** is a singer/songwriter who has recorded three independent albums. This is her first children's book. She says "I wrote Sadie the Bear one afternoon with Sadie at my side soaking up the summer sunshine. Sadie's magical spirit touched me in so many ways; when that kind of magic comes into your life you're obligated to share it with others. Sadie will always be one of my greatest blessings." A Wisconsin Native who has lived in several parts of the country, Kathryn currently makes her home in Rhode Island.

Illustrator **Karen A. Schroeder** moved to Maine from Cape Cod in 1986, she has remained there ever since. "Inspired by the magic of the imagination," Karen enjoys art in all forms and mediums, and has done everything from finger painting to professional sign painting. She currently works at a place she calls "paradise" – Camp Wigwam in Southwestern Maine. This is her first venture into book illustration.

Narrator **Maureen Moran** is an actor and director in Seattle, WA where she has been actively involved in Theatre for over 10 years. She is excited to be breaking into voice-over work as a new artistic endeavor. Maureen's love for the real Sadie the Bear is wonderfully apparent throughout her narration. A Wisconsin Native, Maureen says, "I am a big fan of inspiring, creative children's books and loved being able to lend my voice to this story."

Join Sadie the Bear on her next adventure when she meets a new friend – Chelsea the Sea Dog!

Visit Sadie's Website
www.SadietheBear.com
for details and updates!

Sadie the Bear was flying away
On a beautiful blustery hot summer day
A wayward wind was calling her east
To the sounds and the smells and the sights of the sea
She flew over meadows, treetops and roads
Passing highways and cities and houses below
In the blink of an eye she was ready to land
Her tail wagged with joy as her paws touched the sand
She lay down to rest on the warm soft beach
And the sound of the waves soon lulled her to sleep
Just as her eyes were starting to close
The wind picked up and tickled her nose
On the crest of a wave with a rope in her mouth
Swam a bright yellow dog who was coming about
With a splash and a whoosh she flew through the air
And landed on top of Sadie the Bear
"I'm Chelsea the Sea Dog, don't be afraid,
If you need to be rescued I'll save the day!"

MUSIC BY

KATHRYN PRIESTLEY

If you enjoyed the songs on the *Sadie the Bear* CD
you may want to explore more music by author/singer-songwriter
Kathryn Priestley.

Please log onto her website: ***www.KathrynPriestley.com***
for music samples and information
or contact:

Dancing Dog Productions/Pawper Records
PO Box 113929
North Providence, RI 02911
info@KathrynPriestley.com